FISHING

WRITTEN AND ILLUSTRATED BY
DIANA ENGEL

Macmillan Publishing Company   New York
Maxwell Macmillan Canada   Toronto
Maxwell Macmillan International   New York   Oxford   Singapore   Sydney

Library of Congress Cataloging-in-Publication Data. Engel, Diana. Fishing / written and illustrated by Diana Engel. — 1st ed.   p.   cm.   Summary: When Loretta moves to a new town, she misses her grandfather and the love of fishing they shared. ISBN 0-02-733463-5. [1. Grandfathers—Fiction.   2. Moving, Household—Fiction.   3. Fishing—Fiction.] I. Title. PZ7.E69874Fi 1993   [E]—dc20   91-47705

For Donnie, Kathi, Kimi, and Emi

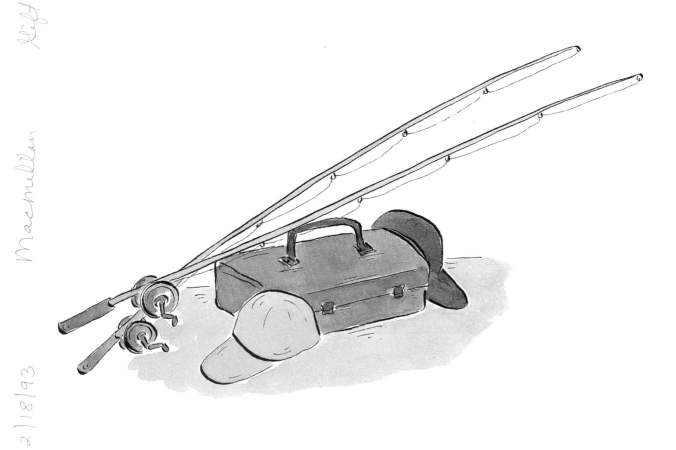

*L*oretta loved to fish.

    She and her grandpa sat together for hours, feeling the warm sun on their shoulders, waiting for the tug on the line.

Waiting was hard work.

"Sh…" whispered Grandpa. "Can you hear the fish?"

Loretta listened carefully. Was that the sound of a thousand fish swimming below the boat? Would one bite the bait on her hook?

Some days were lucky and some days were not.
"Don't you worry," Grandpa would say as he
carried home their empty bucket. "Tomorrow we're
gonna catch the grandaddy of all fish...you wait
and see."

The next day, back in the boat, the waiting began again.

"Sh…" whispered Grandpa. "I can hear the fish."

As the boat bobbed gently in the water Loretta wondered: Would it happen today? Would she feel a tug on the line? Would it happen?

And then it did! A nibble! A tug! A bite! Loretta's hands held on tight, her heart raced, and the line stretched. It seemed the whole world had stopped to listen.

Loretta reeled her line faster and faster. The heavy pull on the end came closer and closer to the surface of the water.

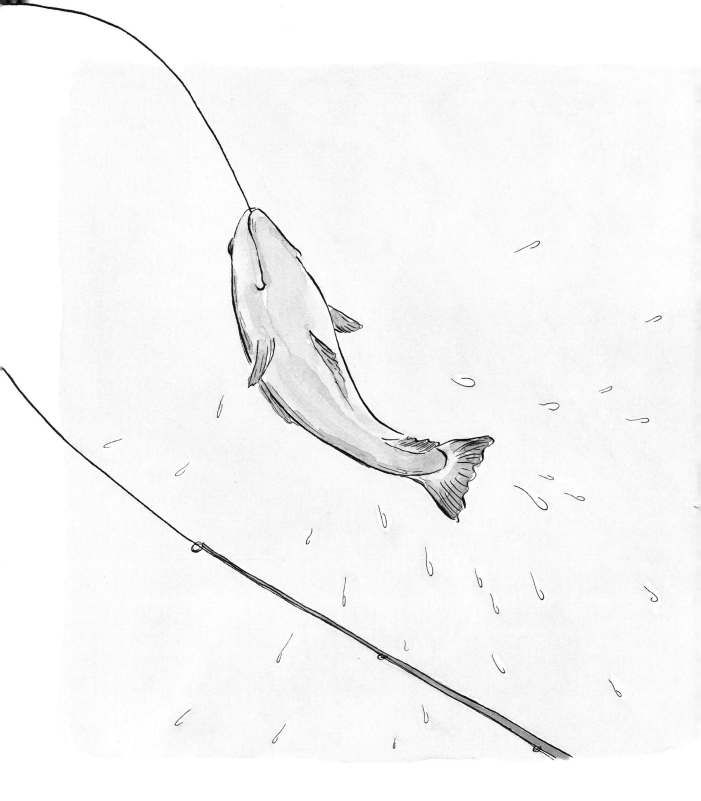

Finally it broke through, flip-flopping in the air
and shining in the sun.

"What did I catch?" yelled Loretta. "What did I catch?"

"A real beaut!" said Grandpa, holding the net. "A real beaut!"

On those lucky days, Loretta's mother cooked up
a special feast for their little family.

"Tomorrow," said Grandpa after dinner, "we'll
catch us another."

Loretta slept soundly, fish swimming through her dreams.

Some days later, Loretta sat with her mother, rocking on the old porch swing. Grandpa watched the sky turn rosy and gold.

"I have something very important to tell you," said her mother.

Loretta waited for the news.

"I've found a new job, a good one," her mother said. "But it's far away, up north. You and I will be moving soon."

"But what about Grandpa?" asked Loretta, trying not to cry.

"We've talked it over," said her mother, "and Grandpa wants to stay here."

"You know me," he said. "Got to be near the
water to be happy."

"So do I!" shouted Loretta, running toward the
dock. "I'll never leave!"

Grandpa followed slowly.

"Don't you worry," he said. "You come on down next summer and we'll fish every single day, rain or shine. We'll catch that old grandaddy fish and keep him as a pet. Better start thinkin' up some good names."

Loretta leaned closer. "I'll miss you, Grandpa,"
she said.

Loretta's new house was small, but it had a little yard in back planted with flowers and tomatoes.

School would start soon and Loretta wondered if she'd make any friends.

The first few days were pretty lonely. Old friends walked together, talking and laughing. Loretta walked home every day by herself.

On the weekend, her mother made Loretta's
favorite dinner, hoping it would cheer her up.

"It tastes better when you catch it yourself," said
Loretta.

Her mother smiled. "Let's call Grandpa," she said.
"How ya doin'?" asked Grandpa.
"Okay," said Loretta in a droopy voice.
"Hey," he said. "I caught a real beaut today, but
it's not the same without you...much too quiet. I
started saying 'sh' to the fish!"

Loretta felt better after hearing Grandpa's voice.
She slept, remembering the warm sun and the
gently bobbing boat.

The next day, on her way home from school, Loretta saw an old paper clip, bent and twisted out of shape. She thought of Grandpa's fish hooks and put it in her pocket.

"I'm going fishing!" she yelled as she raced through the house.

With a bit of string and the old paper clip, Loretta made a fishing line.

She ran outside and sat on the bench in the center of the garden, surrounded by a sea of soil and plants. She threw the line high over the hedges and closed her eyes.

The sun warmed her shoulders. She felt the
bench bob and rock like Grandpa's little boat. She
could hear Grandpa himself whispering to
her.…"Sh…sh…can you hear the fish?"

Loretta smiled to herself. And then she felt…a
nibble! A tug! A bite! What? Her eyes popped open.

"What did I catch?" she said out loud. "What did I catch?"

She ran around the hedge.

There, on the other side, was a little girl, just
Loretta's age.

"What are you doin'?" asked the girl.

"Fishing," said Loretta, blinking.

"Can I do it with you?" the girl asked.
"Sure," said Loretta, still dazed.

The new girl smiled. Loretta smiled back.

Again she could hear her grandpa's voice, this time loud and clear.

"You caught a beaut!" he said. "A real beaut!"